Long ago, Koala and Tree Kangaroo were good friends.
Back then, Koala had a long, furry tail. This is the story of how
Koala came to have a stumpy tail.

One year, there was no rain. All the streams dried up. Water could not be found anywhere.

"Even the leaves on the trees are dying," Koala said to Tree Kangaroo. "We will die too, if it does not rain soon."

"I have an idea," said Tree Kangaroo. "When I was little, there was a very dry season. To find water, my mother dug a hole in a dry streambed. She dug and dug for hours."

"At last, water began to fill the bottom of the hole. There wasn't a lot of water, but there was enough for both of us to have a good drink."

Koala cried, "Let's try that! I can't wait to taste the cool water."

Koala and Tree Kangaroo went to a streambed.
It was as dry as the desert.

Koala whined, "I'm tired and thirsty. You start digging while I rest in this tree. As soon as I get my strength back, I'll dig while you rest."

Tree Kangaroo began to dig. It was hard work, but the thought of the cool water kept him going.

When Tree Kangaroo took a break and looked up, Koala was sound asleep. Tree Kangaroo thought, "When Koala wakes up, he'll be well rested. Then he can take his turn."

So Tree Kangaroo kept on digging.

When Koala woke up, Tree Kangaroo called out, "Now it's your turn. You must do your part."

Koala began to climb down from the tree. But then he cried, "Ouch! I just got a thorn in my foot. You keep digging while I get it out."

So Tree Kangaroo kept on digging. The hole got deeper and deeper, but still there was no water.

"Koala!" yelled Tree Kangaroo. "I am worn out. I need a break."

Again, Koala began to climb down. But this time he called out, "I'm dizzy from lack of water. I must rest a little longer."

Tree Kangaroo was getting mad, but he kept on digging. At last, some water appeared. "Koala, it worked!" he shouted. "Water is slowly filling the hole. Soon there will be enough for both of us."

When Koala heard this, he jumped down and rushed to the hole. He pushed Tree Kangaroo out of his way. Koala stuck his head into the water and began to gulp it down.

Tree Kangaroo was furious. He called out, "Save some for me!" But Koala kept on drinking, and drinking, and drinking.

Tree Kangaroo grabbed Koala's tail to pull him out of the hole. He yanked and yanked. At last, Koala's tail broke off.

To this day, Koala's tail is short and stumpy. And because Koala was lazy and selfish, he also lost a good friend.

About Koalas and Tree Kangaroos

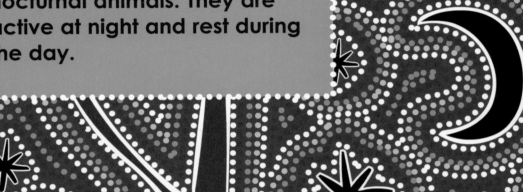

Koalas and tree kangaroos are nocturnal animals. They are active at night and rest during the day.

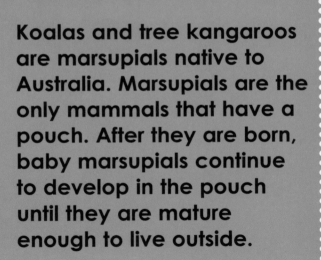

Koalas and tree kangaroos are marsupials native to Australia. Marsupials are the only mammals that have a pouch. After they are born, baby marsupials continue to develop in the pouch until they are mature enough to live outside.

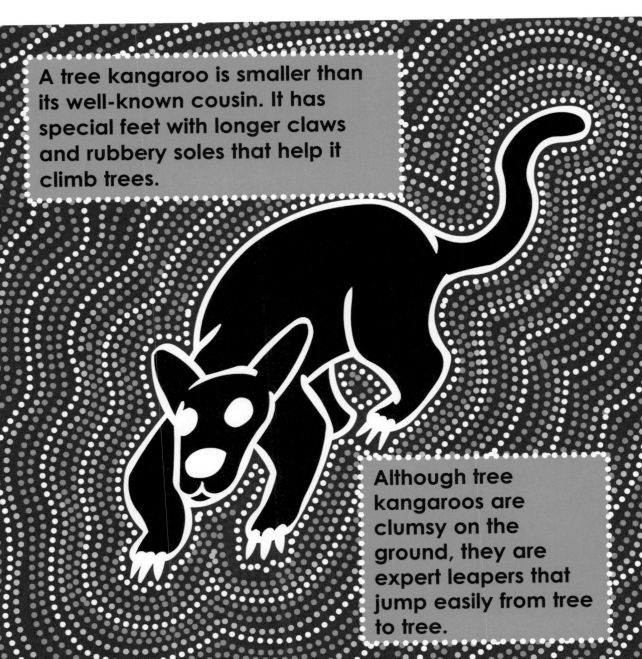

A tree kangaroo is smaller than its well-known cousin. It has special feet with longer claws and rubbery soles that help it climb trees.

Although tree kangaroos are clumsy on the ground, they are expert leapers that jump easily from tree to tree.

Koalas have a tail, but it is really just a short rounded stump.

Although often referred to as "koala bears," koalas are not related to bears at all.

Koalas drink little water but instead find moisture in the eucalyptus leaves that are their primary diet.

Because koalas don't get a lot of energy from their leafy diet, they spend most of their time sleeping or resting in trees. As a result, some call the koala a lazy animal.